ASTERIX AND THE GREAT CROSSING

TEXT BY GOSCINNY

DRAWINGS BY UDERZO

TRANSLATED BY ANTHEA BELL AND DEREK HOCKRIDGE

KNIGHT BOOKS
Hodder & Stoughton

First published in Great Britain 1976 (cased)
by Hodder & Stoughton Children's Books

This edition first published 1979 by Knight Books,
Hodder Dargaud

Fifth impression 1986

Printed and bound in Belgium for Hodder Dargaud Ltd.,
Mill Road, Dunton Green, Sevenoaks, Kent
(Editorial Office: 47 Bedford Square, London, WC1B 3DP)
by Henri Proost & Cie, Turnhout

ISBN 0 340 24714 2

GAULISH VILLAGE

COMPENDIUM

LAUDANUM

AQUARIUM

TOTORUM

ARMORICA

BELGICA

LUTETIA

SPQR

GAUL
(ROMAN CONQUEST)
50 B.C.

CELTICA

PROVINCIA

AQUITANIA

The year is 50 BC. Gaul is entirely occupied by the Romans.
Well, not entirely... One small village of indomitable Gauls still
holds out against the invaders. And life is not easy for the
Roman legionaries who garrison the fortified camps of
Totorum, Aquarium, Laudanum and Compendium...

a few of the Gauls

Asterix, the hero of these adventures. A shrewd, cunning little warrior; all perilous missions are immediately entrusted to him. Asterix gets his superhuman strength from the magic potion brewed by the druid Getafix...

Obelix, Asterix's inseparable friend. A menhir delivery-man by trade; addicted to wild boar. Obelix is always ready to drop everything and go off on a new adventure with Asterix – so long as there's wild boar to eat, and plenty of fighting.

Getafix, the venerable village druid. Gathers mistletoe and brews magic potions. His speciality is the potion which gives the drinker superhuman strength. But Getafix also has other recipes up his sleeve...

Cacofonix, the bard. Opinion is divided as to his musical gifts. Cacofonix thinks he's a genius. Everyone else thinks he's unspeakable. But so long as he doesn't speak, let alone sing, everybody likes him...

Finally, Vitalstatistix, the chief of the tribe. Majestic, brave and hot-tempered, the old warrior is respected by his men and feared by his enemies. Vitalstatistix himself has only one fear; he is afraid the sky may fall on his head tomorrow. But as he always says, 'Tomorrow never comes.'

(BUT LET US LEAVE THESE ICY SEAS, VEILED IN DENSE, IMPENETRABLE MISTS...)

6

THROW OUT THE NET, OBELIX!

AYE, AYE, SIR!

HOW DO WE GET THE NET BACK NOW?

JUST PULL IT IN.

PULL IT IN? BUT I'VE THROWN IT OUT!

YOU MEAN TO SAY YOU DIDN'T TIE IT TO SOMETHING FIRST?

YOU MUST BE CRAZY, THROWING A NET OUT LIKE THAT!

YOU TOLD ME TO THROW IT OUT, SO I DID THROW IT OUT!

I'M A MENHIR DELIVERY-MAN, I AM! NOT A FISHERMAN!

ALL RIGH CALM DOWN. WE'LL JUST HA TO GO BACK FOR ANOTHER NE

THE WIND'S TOO STRONG! WE CAN'T GO ABOUT!

HUH! HE LAUGHS AT ME AND HE CAN'T EVEN SAIL A BOAT!

I DON'T NEED ANY MENHIR DELIVERY-ME GIVING ME ADVICE!

11

YOU SEE? WE HAVEN'T COME TO THE EDGE OF THE SEA, THERE AREN'T ANY MONSTERS, AND THE WINDS DIED DOWN.

WE CAN'T SEE LAND ANY MOR

WE'LL TURN BACK HOME AS SOON AS WE GET A FAVOURABLE BREEZE. WE'VE JUST GOT TO WAIT.

I'M HUNGRY!

THINK OF SOMETHING ELSE.

IF YOU HADN'T TOLD ME TO THROW OUT THE NET, WE COULD HAVE CAUGHT SOME FISH... I'D RATHER EAT A BOAR, OF COURSE.

I SAID THINK OF SOMETHING ELSE... THINK OF YOUR MENHIRS.

WITH THAT SAUCE IMPEDIMENTA MAKES, I COUL EAT A MENHIR... REMEMBER THAT SAUCE?

MMM, YES!... VERY GOOD SPECIALLY WHEN SHE PUTS IN THOSE LITTLE ONIONS AND BITS OF BACON...

ASTERIX! I'M HUNGRY!

I'M HUNGRY TOO! IT'S YOU MAKING ME HUNGRY, GOING ON ABOUT MENHIRS WITH ONIONS!

?

GRRRRR

LOOK!

A SHIP!

WELL, WELL, WELL! IT'S OUR OLD FRIENDS!

SHALL WE GET THEM? SHALL WE GET THEM?

JUST A MOMENT. HOW ABOUT A CHANGE IN THE SCRIPT? IT'S MY BIRTHDAY TODAY... YOU WOULDN'T WANT TO SPOIL MY BIRTHDAY, WOULD YOU? JUST TELL ME WHAT YOU WANT AND THEN GO AWAY THIS ONCE WITHOUT SINKING ANYTHING.

OH, WE'RE ONLY LOOKING FOR A BITE TO EAT!

ASTERIX! LOOK WHAT I'VE FOUND!

WE DON'T WANT TO BE TOO GREEDY; WE'LL LEAVE YOU THIS SAUSAGE. HAPPY BIRTHDAY!

SOON AFTERWARDS...

HAPPY BIRTHDAY TO YOU, HAPPY BIRTHDAY TO YOU...

ALL RIGHT, DON'T OVERDO IT!

CHOP! CHOP!

TIME PASSES...

HERE'S TODAY'S RATION, OBELIX. CHEW IT WELL.

THERE'S STILL A DROP OF RAINWATER IF YOU'RE THIRSTY.

DOGMATIX! YOU GREEDY DOG! YOU'VE SWALLOWED YOUR RATION IN ONE GULP!

WILD BOAR! HEAPS OF WILD BOAR! I CAN SEE THEM! I'M GOING TO GET THEM! COME ON, DOGMATIX!

OBELIX! DOGMATIX! NOOO!

PLIF!

PLOUF!

THEY'RE ABSOLUTELY CRAZY!

PLAF!

I DON'T KNOW WHAT CAME OVER ME... I WAS SEEING BOARS; I WAS EVEN SEEING ROMANS...

LET'S GET BACK ON BOARD OUR...

OUR BOAT!!!

LET IT GO... DOGMATIX AND I WOULD RATHER STAY HERE. PERHAPS THE BOARS WILL COME BACK...

MEANWHILE WE'LL JUST HANG ON TO THIS BRANCH.

BRANCH? WHAT BRANCH?

16

17

THERE AREN'T ANY BEARS NEAR OUR VILLAGE ... SO WHERE ARE WE?

I'M TRYING TO DISCOVER, THE SAME AS YOU.

SNIFF!

WELL, WE'LL EAT THIS BEAR AND AFTER THAT, BY TOUTATIS, WE'LL SEE!

DON'T YOU WANT ANY? THERE'S STILL A BIT LEFT ...

NO ... I'M WONDERING WHERE WE CAN HAVE FETCHED UP ...

SCRUNCH

A LITTLE LATER ...

OH, WELL, LET'S HAVE A REST ... WE'LL SEE LATER

GOOD IDEA!

DOGMATIX HAS PICKED UP ANOTHER SCENT!

OH, GOODY, SOMETHING ELSE TO EAT! I REALLY AM RAVENOUS.

GRRRRRR!

RAVENOUS? YOU'VE ONLY JUST EATEN TWO GOBBLERS, ONE OF THEM STUFFED WITH BEAR.

IT'LL TAKE A LOT OF GOBBLERS AND A LOT OF BEARS TO MAKE ME FORGET THAT APPLE!

ASTERIX! COME AND LOOK! ROMANS!

?

19

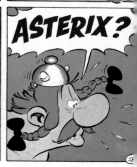

LET'S SEE... ASTERIX NEVER TAKES HIS HELMET OFF EXCEPT TO EAT AND SLEEP...

... AND HE WASN'T EATING, BECAUSE HE WAS WAITING FOR ME AND THE GOBBLERS, AND IF HE WAS ASLEEP HE'D BE HERE... SO SOMETHING MUST HAVE HAPPENED TO HIM.

?!?

PAF!

YOU, ROMAN! WHERE'S ASTERIX?

ASTERIX WOULD KNOW HOW TO MAKE HIM TALK... SO FIRST I MUST FIND ASTERIX!

POF!

SEEK! SEEK, DOGMATIX!

SNIFF! SNIFF!

25

I THINK HE'S CHALLENGING YOU!

YOU DO?

GLUG.
GLUG.

PAF!

I'VE FINISHED MINE.

MY TURN, THEN.

PAFFF!

HOHOHOHOHOHOHOHOH

OON AFTERWARDS...

I THINK HE WANTS US TO STAY HERE.

LOOK, I'M NOT JOINING UP IN THE ROMAN ARMY!

WELL, LET'S ACCEPT. THAT WAY WE MAY FINALLY FIND OUT WHERE WE ARE.

A LITTLE LATER... LET HIM. IT MUST MEAN WE'VE BEEN TAKEN ON AS RECRUITS.

WHO'D HAVE THOUGHT I'D EVER WEAR THE UNIFORM OF A ROMAN MERCENARY?

HAVE YOU NOTICED THE LITTLE CRETAN GIRLS? I WOULDN'T MIND BEING IN THIS CRETE WITH A FEW LIKE THAT...

WELL, DON'T GO BEING INDISCREET HERE.

GOBBLE GOBBLE? WOOF WOOF.

SLAP! SCRUNCH!

28

I'D LIKE TO KEEP THIS AS A SOUVENIR OF OUR DAY'S HUNTING...

ESPECIALLY AS THE IBERIANS SEEMED QUITE IMPRESSED WITH OUR TECHNIQUE!

UGH!

OH, HOW KIND!

?

AHU!

??

GRRRR!

I THINK IT'S HIS DAUGHTER, AND HE'S PLEASED SHE LIKES YOU.

WHAT?!

BONK!

"HEY, THIS FAT IBERIAN GIRL IS FOLLOWING ME AROUND!"

GRRRR!

?

UGH!

TEE HEE HEE!

?

OLÉ!

WHAT DOES THAT CENTURION WANT ME TO DO?

I THINK HE WANTS YOU TO MARRY HIS DAUGHTER!

NO, THANK YOU VERY MUCH! I DON'T WANT TO BE A CENTURION'S SON-IN-LAW!

ANYWAY, I'M TOO YOUNG!

I THINK THE TIME HAS COME FOR US TO START LOOKING FOR OUR VILLAGE AGAIN... I'VE AN IDEA WE'RE A LONG WAY FROM HOME.

WHILE WE WERE HUNTING, I NOTICED THAT WE'RE ON AN ISLAND... WE'LL NEED A BOAT.

I SAW SOME BOATS DOWN BY THE RIVER.

GOOD. TONIGHT WE'LL TRY TO WELSH ON OUR HOSTS!

TWO WELSH? WHAT, WITH ALL THESE CRETANS AND IBERIANS AROUND THE PLACE ALREADY?

THAT NIGHT...

CRACK

HE'S HEARD US!

HANG ON!

GOBBLE!
GOBBLE!
GOBBLE!

UGH!

SOON AFTERWARDS...

THAT WAS A GOOD TRICK!

I SURE HAVE LEARNT A THING OR TWO HOME ON THIS RANGE!

I'VE NEVER SEEN A BOAT LIKE THIS BEFORE!

YES, THAT HOLE TO LET THE WATER IN IS RATHER UNUSUAL.

BLOP!
BLOP!
BLOP!
BLOP!

!

MAYBE HUNTINGSEÅSSEN HÅS SCENTED LÅND....

WHÅT LÅND, HERENDETHELESSEN?

PAT! PAT! PAT!

I DØN'T BELIEVE IN THIS LÅND YØU KEEP ØN ABØUT! NØ ØNE BELIEVES IN IT! THERE ISN'T ÅNY LÅND! WE'RE GØING TØ CØME TØ THE EDGE ØF THE SEÅ AND THEN FÅLL ØFF, BY THØR!

YØU NEVER BELIEVE ÅNYTHING STEPTØÅNSSEN! I'M SURE THERE'S LÅND ÅHEAD! IT MÅY EVEN BE INHÅBITED!

I SHÅLL DISCØVER THIS LÅND, ÅND TÅKE HØME SØME ØF THE NÅTIVES TØ PRØVE IT!

LET'S TURN BÅCK WHILE THERE'S STILL TIME! WHÅT DØ YØU SÅY, HÅRÅLDWILSSEN? ÅND YØU, NØGØØDREÅSSEN? ÅND YØU LØT?

YERSSE!

GRØØ AAÅR

THÅT HØUND ØF YØURS IS BEGINNING TØ ...

LØØK! LØØK, BY ØDIN!

35

LET'S TRY TØ GET ÅCQUÅINTED. I'LL DØ THE INTRØDUCTIØNS. ME HERENDETHELESSEN THE ÅDVENTURØUS...

HIM NØGØØDREÅSSEN THE NUTCÅSE...

YEÅH!

ME STEPTØÅNSSEN SHIFTY-EYES...

ME HÅRÅLDWILSSEN THE INTELLECTUÅL. YØU WHÅT?

I THINK THEY WANT TO KNOW WHO WE ARE.

WELL, LET'S PUT ON THE SHOW WE GAVE THOSE ROMAN COLONIALS AGAIN.

BONG! BONG!

IT'S ALL RIGHT, ASTÉRIX. THEY GET THE IDEA.

TÅP! TÅP! TÅP!

SURE ENOUGH, IT IS A FAST
CROSSING, AND SOON A
THICK FOG COVERS THE
ICY SEA ...

LÅND!

WE'RE BÅCK !
PREPÅRE TØ HÅVE
HONØURS HEÅPED
UPØN YØU !

ØH, THERE YØU ÅRE ÅT
LÅST, HERENDETHELESSEN!
YØU LÅZY BLIGHTER! BY
ØDIN, WHERE THE
NIFLHEIM HÅVE
YØU BEEN ?

IT'S ... IT'S
ØDIUSCØMPÅRISSEN
THE TERRIFYING,
THE CHIEF ØF OUR
TRIBE!

ØF CØURSE IT'S
ØDIUSCØMPÅRISSEN!
DID YØU THINK IT
WÅS Å DEÅR LITTLE
MERMÅID ?

I SÅLUTE YØU, Ø
CHIEF ØDIUSCØMPÅRISSEN!

ÅND
I DØN'T
SÅLUTE YØU!

WHILE WE WERE ÅLL ØUT ØN Å RÅIDING
EXPEDITIØN, MR HERENDETHELESSEN
WENT FØR Å CRUISE!

WE HÅVE PILLÅGED ÅND
BURNT, WE'VE BRØUGHT
BÅCK PLUNDER, SLÅVES,
WHILE YØU...

WHILE I'VE
BEEN DISCØVERING
Å WØRLD!... Å
NEW WØRLD!

41

RIGHT, LET'S HEAR THIS SÅGÅ!

GØ ØN, HÅRÅLDWILSSEN!

UM... ER...

FULL ØF HØPE ÅND CØURÅGE WE SET FØRTH, ØNE MISTY MØRNING IN...

CUT IT SHØRT, YØU FØØL, ØR I SHÅLL CUT YØU SHØRT WITH THIS!

TWO MINUTES LATER...

... TILL BÅCK THIS MØRNING STØP DELIGHTED HEÅR BELØVED CHIEF'S DULCET VØICE STØP

ÅMÅZING! ÅND DØES THIS LÅND LØØK RICH?

SEE HØW WELL-NØURISHED THIS NÅTIVE IS. ÅND THE ØTHER ØNE MÅY SEEM FRÅIL, BUT HE HÅS SUPERHUMÅN STRENGTH!

WØMEN! GERTRUDE! INTRUDE! IRMGÅRD! FIREGÅRD! GET Å FEÅST REÅDY STRÅIGHT ÅWÅY! WE'RE GØING TØ CELEBRÅTE THE RETURN ØF ØUR HERØES ÅND ØUR IMMINENT DEPÅRTURE FØR THE NEW WØRLD!

43

47

PRINTED IN BELGIUM BY
proost
INTERNATIONAL BOOK PRODUCTION